Clashes In Human Life

Dr. Sandip Saha

Ukiyoto Publishing

All global publishing rights are held by

Ukiyoto Publishing

Published in 2022

Content Copyright © Dr. Sandip Saha

ISBN 9789360167844

All rights reserved.
No part of this publication may be reproduced, transmitted, or stored in a retrieval system, in any form by any means, electronic, mechanical, photocopying, recording or otherwise, without the prior permission of the publisher.

The moral rights of the author have been asserted.

This is a work of fiction. Names, characters, businesses, places, events, locales, and incidents are either the products of the author's imagination or used in a fictitious manner. Any resemblance to actual persons, living or dead, or actual events is purely coincidental.

This book is sold subject to the condition that it shall not by way of trade or otherwise, be lent, resold, hired out or otherwise circulated, without the publisher's prior consent, in any form of binding or cover other than that in which it is published.

www.ukiyoto.com

I dedicate my book to every human.

Acknowledgement

1. 'Paying guest' published on pages 60 in Volume XXXIII, 2019 of Peregrine, USA.
2. 'Bleak future' published in VerbalArt, Vol.4, Issue 2, 2020 (Published in May, 2021), India.
3. 'Hypocrisy guides creation' published in W-Poesis, issue 11, July 2020, page- 119,
Romania.
4. 'Corrupt creator' published by W-Poesis, issue 12, Oct 1, 2020, page 119, Romania.
5. 'Devious' published by Verbal Art, Vol. 5, Issue 2, July, 2022, India.
6. 'A new yoga' published by Down in the Dirt, Vol 182, Scar Publication, April, 2021,
USA.

Contents

Undue duel	1
I am ruthless	3
Kill the evil	4
Evil force always makes merry	5
Human vulture	7
Dole of democracy	8
Equality is a misconception	10
Paying guest	12
Mismatch	14
Bleak future	16
Venomous	18
Hodgepodge	20
Sexual appetite	21
Carnal connection	23
Monster's son	25
Murder of mother with a smile	27
Crooked bosses kill organization	29
I am cell phone	31
Family is becoming extinct	33
Human to animal	35
Ugly culture	37
Hypocrisy guides creation	39
Corrupt creator	40
Denouncing big bastard	41
Devious	43
A new yoga	45
About the Author	*47*

Undue duel

There is a lot of fight for equal right
mostly by women against men
or by LGBT against rest.

Usually everybody, be it a person
or any media takes the side
in favour of the demand.

Frankly speaking, even God
does not make
all of us equal.

There is no God incarnation
born as a woman
or as a LGBT.

No man worships the God
as his wife,
woman does.

Perhaps the reason is in such a case
God will not be worshiped
but instead abused.

Even all organs of our body
do not enjoy
equal right.

Body parts like heart, brain
get much more care
as against leg, hand.

No two persons in this world
are equal in capability
and appearance.

Why are you then engaged in the
unending, undue
futile fight?

I am ruthless

I am a man of weird nature
as they say, I don't think so.
I portray God as an oppressor
I want to deactivate It.
It creates man, make them pawns
ask them to dance to Its tunes.
I ask humans do not listen to It
go for one child to ensure extinction
the Tormentor will fail to play
with our lives making it a hell.

I am ruthless to those who betray
act against me after taking all helps
from me many times, show their fangs.
I uproot those in no time
making them toothless down to dust
they cannot afford to challenge me
since I have closed all doors for them.

Kill the evil

The children are innocent
brutal employers are prudent
they exploit due to greed
and abuse them in exchange of bread.

So many laws are made
all remain unused
the government is ineffective
as it does what is lucrative.

The businessmen do business,
give money in election process
politicians award them license
general public pay the expense.

Child labours die early death
without education and proper health
but the bloodsuckers do not leave this path
in order to make the filthy wealth.

Humanity has taken a back seat
let us correct it with all our might.

Evil force always makes merry

Once one of my kin telephoned me
to save a child's life of his relative
arranging her urgent brain operation,
a difficult job but I did it meticulously.

The guy one day fell seriously ill
near and dear gathered
some of them with moist eyes
his sister was crying loudly
everybody was extremely tensed.
In hospital bed he was making
a horrific sound with oxygen mask on
I visited him stood by his side
in the hospital, he was shivering.
He miraculously survived.

The same guy invited us in his daughter's wedding
and left me and my son in lurch half fed overnight
made to sleep in mosquitoes that sucked our blood.

Later when my son and I bought a new flat

to accommodate my son's family
the jealous guy taunted me asking
whether I have driven out my grandson
or grandson has left me?
What a disgraceful question!
I was hurt badly.

Human vulture

Loser can be someone who wants to gain.
Most of the people in the world
err to define what is meant by gain.
They cheat others and feel satisfied.
Selfish people in power are such examples.
I have bitter experience of them.
To fulfil their personal ego and gain
I have seen them to sacrifice the real goal.
Instead of serving the interest of the nation
they even collaborate with foreigners and barter.
The prestige of mother land is sacrificed.
They are elated by a little pat from a foreign hand.
They are basically slave to power and glamour.
Even after doing such hideous act against own country
they feel that it is a tremendous gain for them.

This is their culture inbuilt in their frame of mind.
I tried to fight against these cowards.
They used all their power to silence me.
They threw me in one corner to perish.
Now I really feel I may be loser in material sense
but still I consider these spineless guys are vulture.

Dole of democracy

When the Titanic developed leaks
nobody could plug them, it sank.

Election, election, election….
the power of democracy is on the prowl
prudent politician prey poor people,
poverty does not guarantee honesty
half fed slum dwellers are prime target
they live together like virus
in a filthy surrounding
dole comes as money, liquor, freebies
amusement reaches sky high
beggars become predators overnight

These unearned abundance makes them so mad
they take it for granted that life is to enjoy
that too without paying any price for it,
being drunk at night with fellow rowdies
they wait for prey, catch lonely pair
waiting for bus to reach home
a juvenile predator is pushed forward

to offer a lift in their bus back home
unsuspecting pair get in
the ever-hungry class enjoys upper class flesh
gang rape the girl, torture them brutally
throw them half dead on the road and flee.

The backbone of society is broken by doles
producing goons and encouraging heinous crimes.

Equality is a misconception

I am in meditation all the while
not only sitting and closing eyes
but also, every other moment
while walking, working, waking
discover truths submerged in flow
of ordinary life without investigation.

Women are capable but physically weak
they are raped by boys and men
unlike men who are hardly forcibly
and sexually abused by women-
this perhaps is the reason
why women like to imitate men.

Football, hockey, cricket, wrestling
and many other activities
were started by men and followed
by women to prove themselves equal,
but while availing privilege, protection,
reservation the belief of equality vanishes.

Women are easily victimized by gurus
 luring them to get God's blessings.

They are so afraid of curse and evil
that most of them do whatever guru says
unlike men who are much less in number
to lick the feet of unscrupulous god-men.

I was also initiated by a so-called guru
but found him of no use in the long run.
When I faced many troubles and miseries
he turned blind eyes to me and kept mum.
I stopped donation to his ashram and
threw away his photo that I once worshiped.

Women are unique in themselves
men can never be equal to them.

Paying guest

Last time I saw her
school going girl.
Long ago I used to
visit them at week end
after tiring office work
enjoyed together
her mother liked
me as a brother.
Relatives are rare
at a place far away
from childhood city.
I left my mother
at a young age.
I missed her miserably,
lonely lamenting
longing for her love
like a lotus for lake.
Landed lastly
as a paying guest
on their insistence.

Three long decades
passed, where were you?

Never ever any contact
time rolled over my life
I became bald-headed
about to retire
exhausted after long battle
preparing to go back
to my native place
just as a soldier's return
home after war.

A sudden phone call
from her, now a mother
of a young girl
pressurizing me to accept
her daughter in my house
as a paying guest.
I refused.
The arrogant woman
shouted over telephone
tearing my ear as though
I was bound
to follow her parents.
I was stunned!

Mismatch

A man married two girls
one aggressive,
the other submissive.

First wife was educated,
working, high salaried.
She was beautiful
that attracted many admirers.
But she was too busy
to be available for husband.
Lonely life of the man
hanged heavy.
He had neither admirer
nor he was an achiever.
He was hard working
but his luck was missing.
His wife left her far behind
and became a renowned lady.

One day the poor fellow fell ill
his wife was not around as usual.
Days together he remained
without care as his wife was on tour.

His condition deteriorated.
An unmarried girl was residing
with her old mother next to his house.
She came forward and nursed him,
called a doctor and provided treatment.
He recovered well and survived.

After a while the man fell in love
with the girl who saved his life.
He told his wife to relieve him
as both were a big mismatch.
Soon he married the girl in whom
he found a perfect match.

Bleak future

Man and woman are two halves to sustain life.
But God has given weeds like terrorists....
They cannot help growth of life as they themselves
are depended on others to continue their own lives.

Mankind is drying up vitality of the society in many ways.
Rape, corruption, murder, abetting suicide, depression...
have made the society unliveable.

Woman, on the other hand, is ascending
in education, sports, creativity what not.
But, I am afraid, I foresee an undercurrent spoiler.
Her growth in social fabric is becoming cancerous.

In many countries there are cases
where women are burnt alive after marriage.
Most of them are genuinely oppressive.
But in many occasions the matter is quite different.

Due to so called education, woman has become
career oriented and their earlier role is demeaned.
Now a caring mother and serving daughter-in-law is
replaced by a woman who dumps child in babysitter and
misbehaves with husband, father-in-law and mother-in-law.
She carries a baggage from father's house
which spills arrogance, hatred and disrespect to in-laws.
For her, everything about her parents and their house

is immensely better than what she gets in in-laws' place.
She gradually turns a happy family before son's marriage
to a hell which ultimately ends up to violence or divorce.

Human society will lose the institution of holy marriage in future.
It will run recklessly for some time before total dooms arise.
After all earth took birth one day and also will die another day.

Venomous

The other day
My life sun swayed
From brightness to
Gloomy darkness
I hardly could fathom
Why it so happened?

I took you to America
Your husband with you
Enjoyed sixteen days
From east to west
Niagara, Statue of liberty
To California so fabulous.

You were eager to visit Iceland
I met your desire so difficult
To fulfil in the midst of pandemic
I took the challenge and spent a lot
You enjoyed, sent videos to parents
But coming back you insulted me.

How venomous you are

Call me by slanderous words

Whatever I did for you

Every time you demeaned it

You held your father high

Misbehaving with me time and again.

Hodgepodge

A mother is lying by the side of a
railway track, a baby with her
is seen still sucking her breasts for milk,
he is too small to know her mother is dead.

A woman is married to a guy hardly months ago,
she has an extra marital affair,
at night she cuts off the genitals of husband
when he is in deep sleep, he screams in agony.

A guy pretends to be a monk,
visits disciple's house frequently
to cure ailing man, his daughter
is molested and raped by the guy.

Farmers are hit by drought,
crops fail, they cannot feed
their family, and commit suicide,
governments do little to prevent it.

Is this a peaceful civilized society?
Oh yes, say all including politicians.
They go on cutting ribbons
as everything remains hodgepodge.

Sexual appetite

'A girl at sixteen is most beautiful'
this saying is believed by all.
One girl of this age and her twelve years
cousin lived as sister and brother.

Joint family teaches many good
but in every good there is bad.
The girl and the boy became intimate
all mistook 'they were only affectionate'.

One day the girl became pregnant
the boy was the father of an infant.
He was the youngest father of the country
such sex by humans is derogatory.

One girl of twelve had a charming face.
She had a karate teacher to teach.
The guy taught karate little,
he became a monster after a while.

Assuring the poor-girl a black belt
he met his sexual appetite.
In parents' disbelief she delivered a girl;

the mother of the baby was in peril.

She disclosed the name of the tormentor
but he accused her grandfather as abuser.
The old man was beaten black and blue,
police came rushing for his rescue.

Carnal connection

She studied in the same college
with the guys from same native place
that perhaps bonded them as friends
two boys and a girl
so close that she goes with the guys
a lone lady for a long drive
for fun or mere foolishness!

Many girls do it time and again
surrendering themselves to hungry wolves
as if unaware of the danger to be caught
like a deer surrounded by wild dogs
tearing her flesh apart.

How educated modern girls can be
so unintelligent to fall in the trap!
or they are driven by inherent desire
that drags them for masculine company.
Hundreds of instances come in the news
but these girls always think that
nothing wrong can happen to them.

The hormone is adolescent boys
make them mad like elephant that kills
everybody on its path
till it mates designated darling.
The girl was raped and killed
brutally by the goons,
her body was dumped inside a bush.
The rapists surrendered before the policemen
on advice from their well wishers
to avoid a severe punishment.
Is this friendship?

Monster's son

I was looking at the mirror,
is it me there, my image?

Oh no! I did not find any 'body'
my eyes can't see visible ray
nor x-ray, infrared, ultraviolet
electromagnetic rays as they pass through
my eyes without making any mark.

I see by my mind even closing eyes
and I see plenty of things-
the teenager killed the seven-year
old boy just to delay school exam
as he was afraid of exam, his phobia
murdered the child as if closing a book
he did not like to read any more.

So simple, get a knife and slit his throat
the victim vomited blood, collapsed
died without any resistance.

I could see the ghost of the teenager

brought forward from his previous birth

after his death like a dog, entered into his mother

as a finer body at an incautious moment

of her unethical carnal pleasure with a monster.

Murder of mother with a smile

The guy was the only child
nature could afford to give
they were so unfortunate parents.

Now-a-days when humans
are borrowing sperm or womb
the nature also perhaps has
gone out of stock to provide
affection in some children born!

Mother dreamed and wished
her son could come up in life.
But he failed and did not do
well in college exams.
Worried mother rebuked him,
stopped pocket money
with hope he would fall in line.

That fateful day when his
father went to office
his mother insisted to go to his
college along with him
to know why he fails repeatedly?

The cruel guy gagged his mother
stabbed by a knife several times on her neck
she bled, bled to death.
The monster son wrote with his mother's blood
on the floor, 'I killed her since she was
insisting to go to my college;' and a 'smiley' at the end!!!

Crooked bosses kill organization

Just after reaching the office
I enquired with my colleague
whether he had taken out the product
from the furnace after oxidation.
He informed it was missing,
I ran down towards the plant
came to know that my boss
had given it to his sycophant,
I shouted over the boss
naming him a thief.

Just at that moment
his superior arrived
saw me to do the same.
He became furious at me
and threatened to sack me
the more I tried to say that
my work was stolen and given
to a person who did nothing
to develop the product
except allowing me to work
with the equipment
allotted to his section though

everybody else was entitled to use it
since it was a costly equipment,
the more he became angry
and ordered me not to be present
when the chairman would visit the plant.

The chairman of our institution
arrived and asked others
why I was not present there?
I went on his calling and explained
how I had developed the product.

After that I was not given promotion
such was the character of bosses who
misused the talent of a subordinate
and deprived his growth in career.

I am cell phone

My mother is technology
but I am not born in her womb
brains stimulated her
to produce me without thinking
what I may do once I keep my feet
in this hapless world
that always hankers after new things.

Even a prime minister
does not bother to examine
how judiciously I should be used
he is always in a spree of development
I am taking the advantage of such attitude
and entering into any activity I find
since I am not a sentient being.

Now I am available to everybody
even babies know me
from their tender age I get into them
they like to see videos of kids, cartoons
then come all sorts of video games
that are dangerous to tender minds
and make them addict.

So many fatal cases
are reported in the news
guys and gals while walking on roads
or on railway tracks go on talking in phone
within moments they are run over and killed.
Addicted children are reprimanded by parents
leading to suicide of child or murder of parents.

Family is becoming extinct

Family? Oh no, where is family now?
I mean pure family that has an ethic.
Head of the family has girl friends
his wife has several boy friends
they all have sex and produce children
these children are half-sister or half-brother
purity has vanished from the society.

Now so-called family members are not
having any heart and have mostly a rotten head.
To meet sex, even women now kill husbands,
murdering wives of course are very common.
Every other day newspapers report that for property
a man kills his brother or even entire family,
one woman kills all family members to have
unhindered sex with her paramour.

In some other cases parents go for work
children are dumped in baby-sitters or high and dry
at home where they gradually start doing nonsense
calling friend inside their house and have free sex.

In some countries some family value is still left
children take care of their old parents.
But due to the modern life of extreme competition
many leave their parents and go abroad.

From joint family earlier we got nuclear family
now human society is drifting towards no family.

Human to animal

I find an increasing trend of domestic despair
about six decades back when I was a child
I used to find several siblings in a family
now many do not have any sister and brother
due to economic pressure and competition
couples do not bear more than one child
over and above that both parents are working
who will take care of the child?

Caring a child is a secondary responsibility now
demand of work place is so high
guys and gals cannot do justice to take care of child
home chore is manipulated somehow
most of the time eating outside foods
that are highly detrimental to health
full of cholesterol, trans fat
that make their hearts weak
causing heart ailment in young age.

These were enough reasons to cause despair
but situation is becoming more and more complex
husband and wife are not satisfied with spouse
due to easy availability of opposite sex

they are inclined to enjoy with more partners
this breaks the institution of marriage
everything looks like free for all.

I speculate of a growing free society
where there will be no sanctity of parents
siblings are already partial
half-brother or half-sister
no pure brother or pure sister any more.
Human society is gradually getting abolished
where love is going to be vanished
and replaced by lust and only lust
a society similar to that of animals.

Ugly culture

I encountered your two faces
one male monster and
the other ferocious female
two sides of the same coin
you exhibit your evil existence
make this creation cruel colossal hell
we human always suffer
struggle to face your onslaught
without any weapon with us
endure pain with tears.

When you kidnap women rape them
pierce rod in to their private parts
leaving them bleeding profusely
at a remote location and they die,
when you kill women and children
in the name of freedom fighting
entering their homes with AK 47 rifles
since they do not belong to your religion,
when you bulldoze honest people by power
and steal the fruits of their glittering talent
make them cry in agony with ruined lives
you are that heinous monster on this earth.

When you look so beautiful from outside
enjoy all luxury provided by the able elder
of a joint family as your husband is inefficient
you silently sabotage his glory by treachery,
when you take the help of glamour of your body
flirt to please your boss to climb in career
lose your chastity like a bitch
and cheat your husband,
when you become like a wild wolf
do not do any duty of your family
try to rule over others by temper and crookedness
you are that ferocious female ruining everything.

Hypocrisy guides creation

In my whole life, I am yet to see a moment
which is completely devoid of any fear or anxiety.
When I imagine my fantasy of creation
it appears different from what we have got.
There, I find an ocean of consciousness
from where creation takes shape
and objects created are always aware
of the fact that they are on a voyage, for a change.
Why introduce ignorance when life is formed?
After all, the incarnations of God live in this world
fully knowing who they are and why they have come.
Imposing good and evil in life with latter's predominance
the creator has made us suffer endlessly.
All sorrows and agonies of humanity or other lives
are due to the wilful arrogance of the creator.
If the creator is all powerful
It should make every individual soul
free of any suffering, as It itself is.
It is hypocritical to play with others' miseries
for the sake of Its own enjoyment.

Corrupt creator

Humans are fond of power
most of them want to conquer.
In the process they even smash
whoever comes in their way.

Power blended with selfishness
is a deadly combination
the more it becomes strong
the greater is the damage and harm.

The God is the most powerful
none can stop It from anything
the tsunami washes away, cyclone crashes
earthquake destroys, who can help?

The life is a tale of sorrow and distress
man seeks solace there in vain
for the enjoyment of the Almighty
he lives his life as slave.

The Creator is all powerful
who can stop It from creating life?
But man can certainly stop breeding
to teach the tormentor a lesson, in Its own coin.

Denouncing big bastard

He abuses the God, day and night
nobody likes him for this,
this is not the only thing
to be disliked about him.

He calls the creator big bustard
since it does not have father,
nor it has mother,
as it is never born nor dies.

He is like a mad man
in the wilderness,
no hope for him
in any matter.

He does not care even
the heavy hand of God
the fear of whom
makes people shiver.

He had thrown the photo
of his spiritual guru
to the road since he felt
his guru was his brutal enemy.

Whatever good he does -
helping people in necessity,
sacrificing hard earn money to please others,
go unnoticed, with little praise.

He believes in only his own Self
without which he stops breathing,
move or do anything whatsoever.
What hell will happen to him after death?

Devious

Long ago when you were alone
even time was not with you
I came forward to give you solace
broke your monotony from which
you wanted to flee forever,
suddenly you erupted so violently
that it has produced today's peril
sufferings of all relentless unavoidable
yes, it was I who gave you company
have you forgotten all that you owe to me?

On the contrary, you make tall claims
you think yourself all in all
fear is not there in your vocabulary
you can do whatever you want
you actually are doing all nonsense
deviously riding a mad horse
to unknown destination
you may not be able to choose
still, I am with you to help
but you are so adamant!

You are unbeatable

as you have all weapons
to make others' life hell
but now I have decided
I shall no more be with you
what can you do to me?
Your evil power can only kill me
as a drop of water evaporates from sea
becomes clouds and floats to go far away
I also will vanish but fall as rain drops again.

A new yoga

What is our basic nature?
We are all divine Soul.
Different forms in creation
are evanescent, rushing to die.
I cut an apple it is white inside
but gradually it blackens,
a baby is born so cute
from very next moment
myriad of ways are after the child
to kill making life so uncertain.

Life is nothing but curse
the Creator is the culprit
not only that It through all religions
asks us to love It, the Almighty.
All methods of realization of God
surprisingly emphasize to adore It
but how a tormentor can be hugged
instead, It should be despised
and this forms my new invented
method to achieve salvation.

We should have levity in our thought

love God only to that extent

that we shall not be slave to meet It

and it is not necessary also for us

as we are always divine and free;

for getting rid of body go for extinction.

About the Author

Dr. Sandip Saha

Sandip Saha from India has been awarded with the following awards:
1. Ukiyoto Literary Award "Poet of the year 2022" for the poetry collection of title, "Trial of God"
2. Global Scholars Foundation Bhartiya Sahitya Ratna "Best Poet Writer Award-2022".
3. Poetry Matters Project Lit Prize-2018, USA.

He is a chemical engineer and doctorate (PhD) in metallurgical engineering from India. He has got three awards for his scientific work and 33 publications on his scientific research work including three patents. He has published three collection of poems including "Trial of God" and "Loving women' by amazon.com, one poetry chapbook, "Toast for women", Oxford, UK, 2021 and is published 112 poems in 38 journals including Sheepshead Review, The literary hatchet, In Parentheses, Down in the Dirt, Juked, Origami all USA; in W-Poesis, Romania; in Wingless Dreamer, UK besides in India, Mauritius and in AAWP: Meniscus literary journal, Australia.

www.ingramcontent.com/pod-product-compliance
Lightning Source LLC
LaVergne TN
LVHW041226080526
838199LV00083B/3413